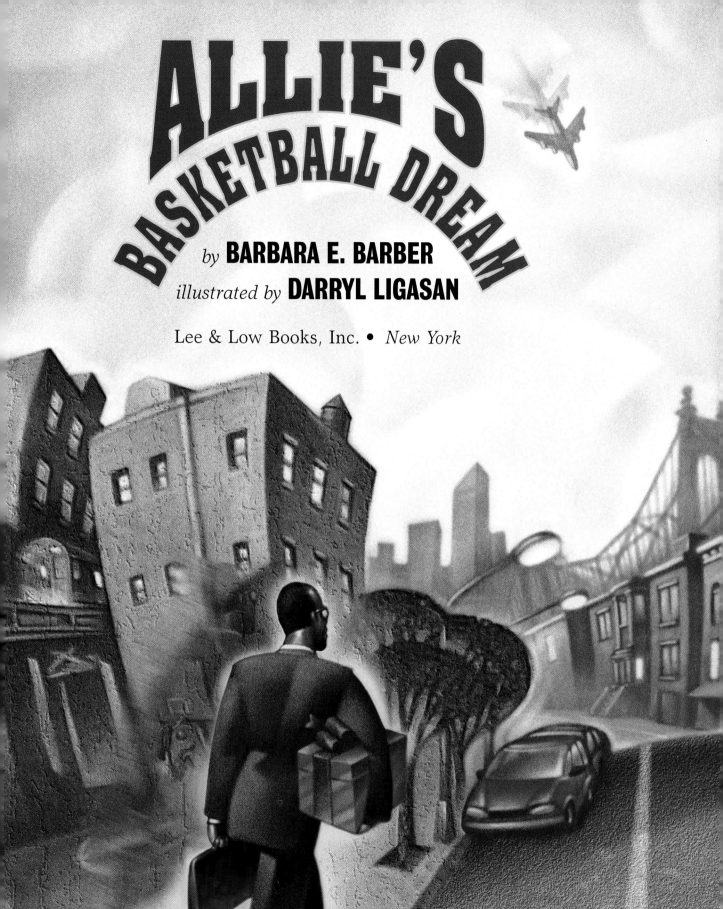

ALLIE'S
BASKETBALL DREAM

by **BARBARA E. BARBER**

illustrated by **DARRYL LIGASAN**

Lee & Low Books, Inc. • *New York*

LEE & LOW BOOKS, Inc., 95 Madison Avenue, New York, NY 10016

Printed in Hong Kong by South China Printing Co. (1988) Ltd.

Book design by Christy Hale
Book production by Our House

The text is set in Garth Graphic.

Illustrator's Note:
The illustrations were created using a variety of traditional and digital techniques.
The sketches were created using pencil and paper. These were transferred into a
computer using a scanner and a digital drawing tablet. The resulting images were
refined in Adobe PhotoShop. Adobe Illustrator was primarily used to create masks
and separate foreground, mid-ground, and background areas. The final illustrations
were then colorized and texture-mapped using a variety of techniques and filters in
Adobe PhotoShop.

10 9 8 7 6 5 4 3 2 1
FIRST EDITION

Library of Congress Cataloging-in-Publication Data
Barber, Barbara E.
  Allie's Basketball Dream/by Barbara E. Barber;
    illustrated by Darryl Ligasan. —1st ed.
      p. cm.
        Summary: Determined in her effort to play basketball, a young
          Afro-American girl gives it one more shot with the help of
            a special friend.
          ISBN: 1-880000-38-5
            [1. Basketball—Fiction. 2. Afro-Americans—Fiction.
              3. Sex role—Fiction.]
                I. Ligasan, Darryl, ill. II. Title.
                PZ7.B2326Al 1996
                  [Fic]—dc20   96-33845
                      CIP AC

*To my beautiful sisters, Saundra (Peaches) Lorraine, Joanie (Kitten)
Louise, and in loving memory of Linda (Cookie) Ray—B.E.B.*

*To my brother Kervin, and my sisters Maria and Carol.
They always found time to play with me—D.L.*

When Allie's father came home from work Friday evening, he brought her a gift. "Because I love you," he said, and kissed Allie on her nose. The gift was something that Allie really wanted—a basketball.

The next day, Allie and her father walked to the playground. Allie loved the sound her new basketball made as she bounced it on the sidewalk. As they passed the firehouse, they waved to Mr. Puchinsky, the fire captain.

"Hi, Domino!" Allie called to the firehouse dog. Domino wagged his tail and licked Allie's basketball when she held it for him to sniff.

At the playground, Allie scanned the basketball courts while her father talked with Mr. Gonzalez, the park monitor. Some older kids already had a game going. All of the players were boys. They hardly ever missed a shot.

"Go ahead and practice, and then we'll shoot baskets together as soon as I get back from taking Aunt Harriet shopping," Allie's father told her. "I'll just be across the street. If you need me, tell Mr. Gonzalez, and he'll come get me."

"Okay," Allie replied.

She waved good-bye and ran to an empty court. She lifted her new basketball over her head and aimed. The shot missed. She aimed again. She missed again.

One of the boys playing in the next court noticed Allie and started to laugh. The others joined in.

"*Boys,*" Allie mumbled. Then she dribbled and bounced. And bounced and dribbled.

Allie's friend Keisha came into the playground with her hula hoop. Keisha saw Allie and held the hoop up. Allie aimed her basketball and.... *Zoom!* Right through the middle.

"Let's play basketball!" Allie said.

"I don't know how," Keisha answered.

"I'll show you."

Keisha twirled her hula hoop. "My brother says basketball's a boy's game."

"Your brother doesn't know what he's talking about," Allie said.

She aimed at an empty trash can. She stepped back a few feet, and took a shot.

Thump! In!

Allie noticed her neighbor Buddy jumping rope with her friend Sheba and another girl. When he missed he ran off to join some other kids who wanted to use his volleyball.

"Hi, Allie!" Sheba called. "Is that your basketball?"

"Yep, my dad gave it to me. Want to shoot some baskets?"

"Maybe later," Sheba replied. "Want to jump double-dutch?"

"Maybe later," Allie said.

Allie pretended she was playing soccer. She kicked the ball and chased it. Then she looked up at the basket, aimed, and shot. The ball struck the backboard, then the rim, and bounded off.

Julio, who was in Allie's class at school, whizzed by on his skateboard. He made a sharp turn when he noticed the new basketball.

"Wow!" Julio exclaimed. "Is that yours?"

"Yes," said Allie proudly. "Let's shoot some baskets!"

Julio looked at Allie, his eyes wide. "You must be kidding!" he said. "Me shoot baskets with a girl? No, thanks!" He laughed and skated away.

Allie heaved a sigh and eyed the basket. She took another shot. The ball circled the rim and fell off. She heard some of the boys in the next court chuckle. She tried again. And again.

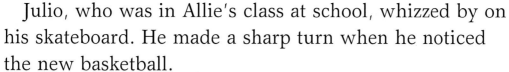

Allie sighed again and plopped down on a bench. Buddy walked over, bouncing his volleyball. "What's up?" he asked. "Something wrong with your basketball?"

"Well..." Allie hesitated.

"I'll trade you my volleyball for it! It's smaller and lighter— it'll be easier for you to play with."

"I don't know," Allie said.

Buddy reached into his pocket. He took out a miniature sports car, two quarters, and some grape bubble gum—Allie's favorite. "You can have these *and* my volleyball for the basketball," he said.

Allie thought it over. She remembered the first time her father took her to a basketball game at Madison Square Garden. She loved it all: The noise of the crowd, the bright lights on the court, and especially the slam-dunks the players made look so easy! She knew right then and there that one day, she would be a professional basketball player, too...

Allie hugged her basketball close. "No way I'm getting rid of this ball! It's a gift from my dad. Someday I'm going to be the best basketball player ever!"

"Well," Buddy snorted, "some guys think girls shouldn't be playin' basketball."

"That's dumb!" Allie bounced her ball. "My cousin Gwen plays on one of the best high school teams in her state. She's won more than ten trophies!"

Buddy looked surprised.

"Some girls think boys shouldn't be jumping rope," Allie continued. "They think boys are no good at it. That's dumb, too."

Buddy unwrapped two pieces of gum. "Want some?"

Allie and Buddy blew huge purple bubbles. They popped their gum so loud that Domino ran over to investigate. He pranced right up to Allie and sniffed her basketball.

"Wanna play basketball, Domino? Come on, boy, let's play!"

Domino ran alongside Allie as she dribbled and bounced. Laughing, Allie turned toward the basket, and took a long-distance shot. The ball brushed against the backboard, rolled around the rim, and dropped in!

Buddy jumped up from the bench. "Nice shot, Allie!" he yelled, and ran to retrieve the ball.

"Thanks," Allie said, beaming.

Julio saw the shot, too. So did Sheba. They both hurried to the center of the court.

"Here!" Allie and Julio and Sheba called to Buddy almost in one voice.

Buddy dribbled the ball, then passed it to Allie. She took a shot and missed.

"Don't worry, Allie!" Buddy yelled. Julio and Sheba each shot and missed. Allie caught the ball and dribbled closer to the basket. *I can't wait to show Dad what I can do,* she thought.

Up, up went the ball. It didn't touch the backboard. It didn't touch the rim. It didn't touch anything.

Zoom! In!

The older boys in the next court applauded. Mr. Gonzalez whistled. Domino barked. Above all the noise rose a familiar voice—Allie's father.

"That-a-girl!" he shouted. "Hooray for Allie!"